Grandma Brown's Three Fine Pigs

~ based on a true story

With thanks to my father 'Norman'

A

Book

Published by Storysack Ltd.
Resource House, Kay Street,
Bury BL9 6BU

ISBN 0-9537099-7-3

Printed in the UK
by
South Western Printers, Caerphilly, Mid Glamorgan CF83 2RZ

Grandma Brown lived in a quiet
Shropshire village with her grandson Norman.
Their home was a large cottage with a front garden
full of flowers and fruit bushes. At the back was an orchard
and it was here that chickens and three fine pigs were kept.

Each morning, before breakfast, Grandma Brown could be heard calling to her hens.

"Here, chuck chucks!" she would cry as she shook their food tin.

They would scuttle out from their nesting boxes in search of grains of corn as Norman collected the golden brown eggs they had laid.

The hens were not the only ones in search of food!
As soon as she began calling, three pink snouts would be
seen above the pigsty gate in the hope of a treat of corn and
Grandma Brown would usually spoil them with a handful each.
They then had to wait until after lunch when they were fed with
scraps from the kitchen and a bucket of special pig feed.

One particular morning, however,
Grandma Brown was to be in for
a shock. Three pink snouts
did not appear above the pigsty
gate as they usually did. In fact
there were no pigs at all. They had
escaped through a small hole they
had made in the fence.

"Norman, Norman!" cried Grandma Brown.
"Quickly - my three fine pigs have escaped,
hurry up and see if you can catch them!"

Norman ran as fast as he could down Spring Bank Lane. Mr Davis was standing in the gateway of his field.

"Mr Davis, Grandma Brown's three fine pigs have escaped. Have you seen them?" asked Norman.

"No, can't say I have, but something has upset the bull. Just look at him!" said Mr Davis.

Norman hurried down Stoppers Hill, where
Mrs Edwards was trimming her front hedges.

"Mrs Edwards, Grandma Brown's three
fine pigs have escaped. Have you seen them?"
asked Norman.

"No, I certainly haven't, but something has startled my
ponies in the paddock. Just look at them!" she said

Norman climbed the stile
and took the short cut across
the fields by the Bellan Brook.
He could see Mr Evans polishing the
brass lanterns outside the village pub.
"Mr Evans, Grandma Brown's three fine pigs
have escaped. Have you seen them?" asked Norman.
"Why no, I'm afraid I haven't, young man, but
something has excited those dogs, they won't stop barking!"

On the other side of the
road, gazing at the village
pond, was the Reverend Douglas
Morgan. "Reverend Morgan,
Grandma Brown's three fine pigs
have escaped. Have you seen them?"
asked Norman.
"No, my boy, I haven't, but something has
disturbed those ducks from their nests."

Norman made his way along the lane that led to the chapel. Mrs Jones was hanging out washing in her front yard.

"Mrs Jones, Grandma Brown's three fine pigs have escaped. Have you seen them?" asked Norman.

"I can't say I have, but something has stirred up my young ones. I can't control them!" she sighed.

Norman made his way to the crossroads,
where he caught sight of his headmaster, Mr Thomas.
He could hardly believe his eyes; Mr Thomas was chasing
sheep around the school playground!
"Mr Thomas, sir, I'm sorry to disturb you, sir, but Grandma
Brown's three fine pigs have escaped. Have you seen them?"
he asked nervously.
"No I haven't, but something has opened the paddock gate and let
those sheep out. They've already eaten their way through a row of
lettuce in the school garden!" he shouted angrily.

Norman decided to slip away and leave Mr Thomas to it, before he got into even more trouble. He hurried back up the hill to 'The Beeches' where he could see Miss Potter through the large gates to her house. She was calling to something high up in a tree.

"Miss Potter, ma'am, Grandma Brown's three fine pigs have escaped. I don't suppose you've seen them?"

"No Norman, I have not, but something has frightened my cats. They won't come down from that tree!"

Norman thought he would try one last place, the post office. When he arrived, Mr and Mrs Ellis were outside.

"Mr and Mrs Ellis, Grandma Brown's three fine pigs have escaped. Have you seen them?" asked Norman hopefully.

"No I'm afraid we haven't. We've had our hands full trying to catch these two rascals. Something trampled through their ropes and let them loose!" replied Mrs Ellis.

This was Norman's last hope.
He didn't know where else to look.
Just at that moment, Sid Price came
running towards him waving.

"Norman, Norman, I've just seen Grandma
Brown's three fine pigs. They've gone through
the hedge into Mrs McCarthy's field!"

They ran to the hole in the hedge and
peered through. Norman could hardly
believe his eyes. The field was full
of pigs! How were they ever going
to find Grandma Brown's?

Sidney ran back to tell Grandma Brown
whilst Norman guarded the hole.
Before long she came trotting
up the lane carrying a large
blue tin.

"How are we going to find them,
Grandma?" asked Norman.

"Don't worry, I think I have
just the thing!" she said.
Grandma Brown began to
shake the tin and call out.

"Here, chuck chucks! Here,
chuck chucks!"

Sidney made a face at Norman.
"Has she gone mad?" he whispered.
Norman shrugged his shoulders, but to their
amazement three pink snouts appeared through
the hole and out trotted Grandma Brown's three fine pigs!

"There, I thought it would work!" said Grandma Brown with a wide grin on her face.
Each of the pigs was rewarded with a handful of corn and they then proceeded
to follow her all the way home, with Norman following behind.

Soon the three fine pigs were safely back in their pigsty,

the hens settled into their nesting boxes,

the bull was grazing peacefully,

the ponies were safely in their stables,

the ducks had returned to their nests,

the dogs were sleeping in their baskets,

the sheep were huddled in their paddock,

Mrs Jones' children were all tucked up in bed,
(well almost!)

Miss Potter's cats were curled
up on her lap,

the goats were tethered tightly,

Grandma Brown was knitting in her rocking chair, and Norman...

...was asleep in the gooseberry patch!

The End

1 bull

2 goats

3 pigs

4 children

5 dogs

6 cats